This book belongs to ...

....

OXFORD
UNIVERSITY PRESS

Great Clarendon Street, Oxford, OX2 6DP,
United Kingdom

Oxford University Press is a department of the University of Oxford.
It furthers the University's objective of excellence in research, scholarship,
and education by publishing worldwide. Oxford is a registered trade mark of
Oxford University Press in the UK and in certain other countries

Ouch!, The Monster Hunt first published in 2006
Teds in Beds, The Duckling first published in 2014
This edition published in 2014

ISBN: 978-0-19-831025-9

1 3 5 7 9 10 8 6 4 2

Paper used in the production of this book is a natural, recyclable product made
from wood grown in sustainable forests. The manufacturing process conforms
to the environmental regulations of the country of origin.

Acknowledgements;
Series Editors: Kate Ruttle and Annemarie Young

READ WITH
Biff,
Chip &
Kipper

Ouch!
and Other Stories

OXFORD
UNIVERSITY PRESS

Tips for Reading Together

Children learn best when reading is fun.

- Talk about the title and the picture on the front cover.
- Look at the *j, x, sh, ch, qu, th* and *ing* words on page 8. Say the sounds in each word and then say the word (e.g. *j-o-b, job*).
- Read the story and find the words with the letters *j, x, sh, ch, qu, th* and *ing* in them.
- Do the fun activity at the end of the story.

Children enjoy re-reading stories and this helps to build their confidence.

Have fun!

After you have read the story, find the red button in every picture.

The main sounds practised in this book are 'j' as in *job*, 'x' as in *fix*, 'sh' as in *shock*, 'ch' as in *check*, 'qu' as in *quick*, 'th' as in *them* and 'ing' as in *missing*.

For more hints and tips on helping your child become a successful and enthusiastic reader look at our website www.oxfordowl.co.uk.

Teds in Beds

Written by Roderick Hunt
Illustrated by Nick Schon,
based on the original characters
created by Roderick Hunt and Alex Brychta

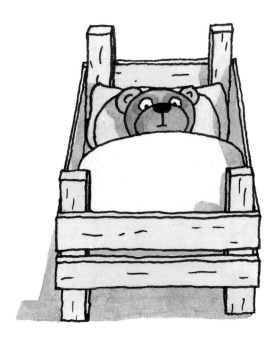

OXFORD
UNIVERSITY PRESS

Read these words

job	fi**x**
miss**ing**	**ch**ill
shock	**qu**ick
check	**th**em

Ruff the pup got Big Ted.

She ran off with him.

It was a job getting Ruff to let go.

Big Ted had a rip on his tum
and a cut on his leg.

Kipper was upset.

He put Big Ted to bed.

Kipper fell asleep.

This ted had a leg missing.

That ted had a rip in his tum.

Kipper had ten teds to fix.

19

He put all of the teds to bed.

Kipper got up. Big Ted was
mended! Gran did it.

A big hug for Big Ted . . .

... and a big hug for Gran.

Talk about the story

Spot the difference

Find the five differences in the pictures of the injured ted.

(Answer to spot the difference: tear drop, 'v' on arm, wheel, stripe on trousers, red cuff)

Tips for Reading Together

Children learn best when reading is fun.

- Talk about the title and the picture on the front cover.
- Identify the letter pattern *ing* in the title and talk about the sound it makes when you read it.
- Look at the *sh*, *ch*, *qu* and *ing* words on page 30. Say the sounds in each word and then say the word (e.g. *qu-a-ck, quack*).
- Read the story and find the words with the letters *sh*, *ch*, *qu* and *ing* in them.
- Do the fun activity at the end of the story.

Children enjoy re-reading stories and this helps to build their confidence.

Have fun!

After you have read the story, find the frog in every picture.

The main sounds practised in this book are 'sh' as in *shock* and *rubbish*, 'ch ' as in *check*, 'qu' as in *quack* and 'ing' as in *duckling*.

For more hints and tips on helping your child become a successful and enthusiastic reader look at our website www.oxfordowl.co.uk.

The Duckling

Written by Roderick Hunt
Illustrated by Nick Schon,
based on the original characters
created by Roderick Hunt and Alex Brychta

OXFORD
UNIVERSITY PRESS

Read these words

shock   rubbish

quack   duckling

quick   check

Wilma had a shock.

The pond was a mess.

Dad put the rubbish in the bin.

Wilma fed the ducks.

But a duckling was missing.

The duckling was stuck.

It had its leg in a bag.

The bag was filling up.

The duckling was sinking.

Wilma was upset.

Dad got the net.

Dad went into the pond.

Dad put the duckling into the net.

They got the bag off the duckling.

Dad was wet!

They put the duckling
back into the pond.

Talk about the story

What was wrong with the duckling?

Why was Wilma upset?

What did Dad do?

What creatures have you helped?

Spot the difference

Find the five differences in the pictures of Dad.

(Answer to spot the difference: net, buttons, collar, pocket, bottom edge of yellow top)

Tips for Reading Together

Children learn best when reading is fun.

- Talk about the title and the picture on the front cover.
- Look through the pictures together and discuss what you think the story might be about.
- Read the story together, pointing to the words and inviting your child to join in.
- Give lots of praise as your child reads with you, and help them when necessary.
- Do the fun activity at the end of the story.

Children enjoy re-reading stories and this helps to build their confidence.

Have fun!

After you have read the story, find the scorpion in every picture.

This book includes these useful common words:

coming girl was went

For more hints and tips on helping your child become a successful and enthusiastic reader look at our website www.oxfordowl.co.uk.

Ouch!

Written by Roderick Hunt
Illustrated by Alex Brychta

OXFORD
UNIVERSITY PRESS

Floppy was dreaming that
he was in the desert.

It was hot in the desert.

The sand was hot.
"Ouch!" said Floppy.

Floppy saw a girl on a horse.

The girl was Biff!

"Quick! Come with me,"
said Biff.

"A sandstorm is coming."

The wind blew the sand.

Biff put Floppy on the horse.

The horse went fast.

"Go faster!" said Biff.

"The sandstorm is coming!"

The horse went faster.

"Ouch!" said Floppy.

The horse stopped.
Oh no!

Floppy flew off the horse.

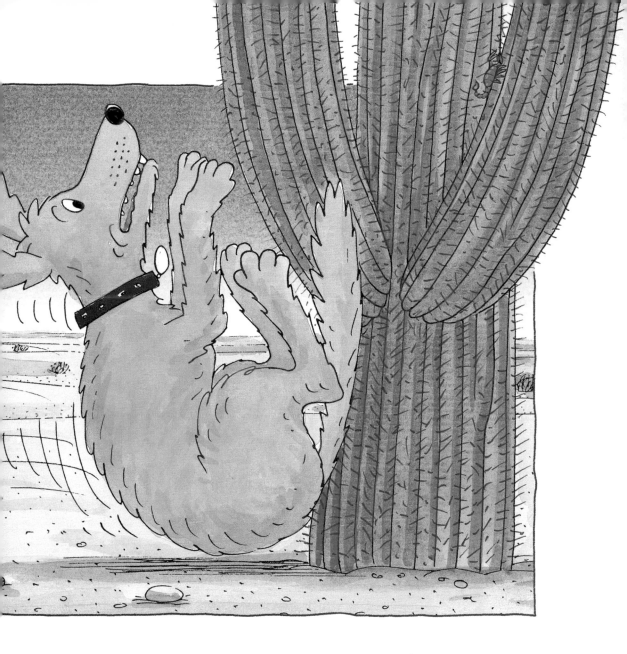

"Ouch!" said Floppy.

"Oh! There's my cactus,"
said Biff.

Talk about the story

Why do you think this story is called 'Ouch!'?

Why did Biff make the horse go faster?

Why isn't it a good idea to touch a cactus?

What do you dream about?

Picture puzzle

How many things can you find beginning with the
same sound as the 'c' in cat?

(Answer to picture puzzle: cactus, cake, candle, car, carrot, caterpillar, cup)

Tips for Reading Together

Children learn best when reading is fun.

- Talk about the title and the picture on the front cover.
- Look through the pictures together and discuss what you think the story might be about.
- Read the story together, pointing to the words and inviting your child to join in.
- Give lots of praise as your child reads with you, and help them when necessary.
- Do the fun activity at the end of the story.

Children enjoy re-reading stories and this helps to build their confidence.

Have fun!

After you have read the story, find the mouse in every picture.

This book includes these useful common words:

children   come   saw   went

For more hints and tips on helping your child become a successful and enthusiastic reader look at our website www.oxfordowl.co.uk.

The Monster Hunt

Written by Cynthia Rider
Illustrated by Alex Brychta,
based on the original characters
created by Roderick Hunt and Alex Brychta

OXFORD

UNIVERSITY PRESS

Gran took the children on
a monster hunt.

Biff saw some monster
footprints.

Chip saw a monster glove,
and . . .

Kipper saw the monster!

"Come on," said Gran.

"Let's get that monster!"

The monster ran.

It ran up the hill.

It ran into the mill ...
and hid.

"Come on," said Chip.

"Let's get that monster!"

They went into the mill.

"Ssh!" said Gran.

"I can see the monster's tail."

Gran pulled the monster's tail.

"Got you!" she said.

"AARGH!" said the monster.

Crash! went a sack.

Crash! went the monster.

The monster looked at the
children. "Help!" he said.

"Monsters!"

Talk about the story

Why do you think Gran and the children went on a monster hunt?

How did the children know which way the monster had gone?

How would you feel if you got covered in flour?

Would you like to go on a monster hunt? What would you do if you caught the monster?

Picture puzzle

Match the monster to its shadow.

(Answer to picture puzzle: monster shadow 2)

Read with Biff, Chip and Kipper
The UK's best-selling home reading series

Phonics   First Stories

Level	Phonics	First Stories
Level 1 Getting ready to read	Kipper's Alphabet I Spy Chip's Letter Sounds Biff's Wonder Words Floppy's Fun Phonics	Get On Floppy Did This! Up You Go Six in a Bed
Level 2 Starting to read	I am Kipper Cat in a Bag The Red Hen The Fizz-Buzz	Funny Fish Silly Races! The Snowman Dad's Birthday
Level 3 Becoming a reader	Such a Fuss Shops The Sing Song The Backpack	Poor Old Rabbit I Can Trick a Tiger Super Dad Floppy and the Bone
Level 4 Developing as a reader	Wet Feet The Moon Jet The Red Coat Quick! Quick!	Missing! The Raft Race Dragon Danger The Spaceship
Level 5 Building confidence in reading	Egg Fried Rice Craig Saves the Day Seasick Dolphin Rescue	Hungry Floppy Husky Adventure Trapped! Looking after Gran
Level 6 Reading with confidence	Gran's New Blue Shoes Ice City Save Pudding Wood Uncle Max	Hairy-Scary Monster Mountain Rescue The Lost Voice Secret of the Sands

Phonics stories help children practise their sounds and letters, as they learn to do in school.

First Stories have been specially written to provide practice in reading everyday language.

Read with Biff, Chip and Kipper Collections:

 Up You Go and Other Stories

 Six in a Bed and other stories

 Funny Fish and Other Stories

 The Fizz-Buzz and Other Stories

 Floppy and the Bone and other stories

 I Can Trick a Tiger and other stories

 The Moon Jet and Other Stories

 Dragon Danger and Other Stories

2 Phonics and 2 First Stories in every collection

Phonics support

Flashcards are a really fun way to practise phonics and build reading skills. **Age 3+**

My Phonics Kit is designed to support you and your child as you practise phonics together at home. It includes stickers, workbooks, interactive eBooks, support for parents and more! **Age 5+**

Read Write Inc. Phonics: A range of fun rhyming stories to support decoding skills. **Age 4+**

Songbirds Phonics: Lively and engaging phonics stories from Children's Laureate, Julia Donaldson. **Age 4+**

Help your child's reading with essential tips, advice on phonics and free eBooks
www.oxfordowl.co.uk